AS CLEAR AS NIGHT

AS CLEAR AS NIGHT

EDGAR J. HERN

Publisher's Cataloging-in-Publication Data

Names: Hern, Edgar J., author.
Title: As Clear As Night / by Edgar J. Hern.
Description: Las Vegas, NV: Amazon KDP, 2025.
Identifiers: LCCN: 2025905086 | ISBN: 979-8-9928840-4-3
(paperback) | 979-8-9928840-5-0
(ebook)

Subjects: LCSH Psychic ability--Fiction. | Teleportation--Fiction.
| Crime--Fiction. | Science
fiction. | Horror fiction. | BISAC FICTION / Science Fiction /
General | FICTION / Horror /
General
Classification: LCC PS3608 .E76 C54 2025 | DDC 813.6--dc23

AS CLEAR AS NIGHT

Wednesday, March 17, 2004. 1:35 a.m.

The silence in the opulent study was stifling, broken only by the faint rustle of gloved hands rifling through a sea of documents. Moonlight filtered through the grand arched window, casting a pale glow on the mahogany desk and the walls lined with leather-bound books. Behind the black ski mask, Alex Blackwell's piercing blue eyes darted from one sheet to the next until, at last, a slip of paper seemed to glow beneath his touch—the elusive bank lockbox number belonging to a New Jersey lottery winner. His lips curled into a wicked smile as he scribbled the information onto a notepad. Then, without a sound, his body began to shimmer and dissolve, fading into the shadows as if he had never been there at all.

Reappearing in the driver's seat of his car, Alex cast one last glance at the millionaire's Villa Grande, its grandeur bathed in ethereal moonlight. The engine roared to life, and he shifted into gear. Feeling the thrill pulse through him, he pulled off the mask to reveal a cunning smile. With his plan now in motion, the promise of a life-changing fortune lay just within his reach.

The air was cold enough to warrant fuzzy wool gloves and scarves that wrapped around twice. Swaying gently like a lullaby in the breeze, the trees tickled the black clouds to a gentle rumble. Light rain fell across central Long Island as a storm raced through the East Coast states. Alex parked his white coupe at the intersection of Jerusalem and Eastern Avenues, across from Province Security Bank. Its proximity to the Seaford-Oyster Bay Expressway was ideal, serving as a quick getaway route.

Having slipped his fingers into thin, nonslip leather gloves, he pulled the ski mask over his head and peered through an 80-millimeter angled spotting scope. The scope's objective lens let in 77% more light than a standard 60-millimeter, delivering sharper resolution through the gloom. From the strip mall parking lot, he could see the vault through the bank's glass doors. After waiting for a teller to exit, he watched as she carefully closed the heavy door without letting it latch before clearing. In an instant, the scope gave way to gravity and bounced twice before settling onto the car's red leather seat.

Alex materialized safely inside the vault in a sitting position, relieved he hadn't landed on the pelvic injury from his last job. It was chilly, and the teller's perfume lingered in the air. He stood quickly, moving toward the appropriate lockbox as ringing phones and distant voices filtered through the partially closed door. Ignoring the blinking red light on the surveillance camera, Alex reached into his leather jacket pocket and pulled out a pouch with a ball-peen hammer and a center punch. But before he could punch the double-lock mechanism, the door behind him slid open again. Shocked at the interruption of what should have been a swift in-and-out job, he glanced over his shoulder and dropped both tools.

The manager gasped at the sight of him, her tattooed eyebrows arching above thick-framed glasses. For a moment, they locked eyes, frozen in mutual hesitation. Then a bulky key chain slipped from her trembling fingers, clattering against the tile. Fear seized her throat, stifling a scream. Her legs buckled as the masked man bolted toward the door. She slammed against the wall and collapsed in a heap onto the cold tile. Whether he shoved her or she fell on her own was never clear.

Alex's heart raced as he vaulted over the counter and sprinted past the customers lined up between him and freedom. *This was not part of the plan,* he thought, his thudding footsteps echoing off the marble walls.

"It's a bank robber!" A woman's piercing scream shattered the sudden silence, triggering a wave of panic. Every eye turned toward the masked man.

To create a diversion, Alex shoved a few startled patrons against the divider ropes. Brass posts clanged as several people toppled while he made a beeline for the glass doors.

Slumped over a check desk, the security guard leaped into action. "Stop!" he shouted, drawing his gun as he darted across the lobby. At the sight of a brandished weapon, more customers screamed and dove for the relative safety of the floor.

Thinking he could reach his car without having to clear, Alex dashed out of the bank, his heart tripping in his chest. Several customers walking up the sidewalk ducked and ran for cover as he bolted past.

The guard flung the glass door open and aimed his gun, one delicately quivering finger on the trigger.

Rain pounded the asphalt as Alex ran mindlessly into the street. A blast from a truck's horn drained the blood from his face. He froze—staring at a fuel tanker bearing down on him. His breath caught. Spotting his car across the street, he quickly envisioned himself behind the steering wheel. With a deafening roar, the truck surged forward, missing his face by mere inches before he cleared.

With adrenaline surging, the security guard's trembling finger tightened—jerking the trigger before thought could intervene. The bullet pierced the truck's front tire, unleashing 105 PSI in a deafening blast.

Instinct took over as the driver slammed on the air brakes and yanked the steering wheel hard left, sending the tanker careening sideways. It growled like a slain dragon, grinding through traffic and gouging deep ruts into the asphalt. With a violent crack, a utility pole snapped under the truck's onslaught and sent live wires snaking onto the pavement. Two cars that skidded into the tank ripped through the metal body, spewing hundreds of gallons of fuel onto the street. One of the fallen power lines swayed like a cobra dancing to the tune of a pungi, spitting sparks each time it hit a puddle.

The driver hauled himself through the window, gripping the side-view mirror for support. A trickle of blood from a cut on his forehead ran down his nose, but he didn't notice. The door panel bent under his weight. As he stood gasping for air, his heart raced like a wild stallion. Fuel thickened the air, its sharp scent mixing with the sight of twisted wreckage below. His thoughts scattered as he assessed the damage, trying to figure out what to do next. It had all happened so fast. He was sure he'd struck the man. And those eyes! Those panic-stricken eyes were an image he would never forget! An icy chill ran down his spine when he noticed sparks flying from a severed power line.

Still locked in its territorial dance, the cobra plunged into the rushing gasoline stream. "Holy shit!" he cried. The explosion rattled the entire block. A civilian who jumped out of his car to help was blasted backward twenty feet. Windows shattered in adjoining buildings as metal fragments from the tanker skewered nearby brick walls, vibrating to a standstill.

When Alex peeled off his ski mask, his normally confident face was pale and damp. His head whirled, and his hands trembled. Breath tore through his burning lungs, each inhale scraping like gravel. Disturbed by the havoc he had caused, Alex watched the inferno in the rearview mirror as he drove down Jerusalem Avenue. This near-death incident served as a stark reminder of his many brushes with death. Yet, none were as terrifying as when he first discovered his ability to clear.

✳ ✳ ✳

Saturday, July 1, 1972.

Alex peered into the freezer, then the refrigerator, his throat parched. The glass of milk did nothing to quench his nagging thirst, leaving him craving something cold enough to freeze the sweat on his brow. He imagined icy water cascading down his body, a chilling waterfall from a towering cliff. His mother's voice echoed from the living room as he rummaged for the perfect drink.

"Try the orange juice. It's fresh!" Melissa called out.

Or was it refreshing? He dismissed the uncertainty, focusing on his mission, and reached down for the orange juice. Noticing the dewy carton, he tightened his grip as he lurched up—forgetting the freezer was still open. His skull struck the door with a bone-jarring crack, shaking the refrigerator to its core. Searing pain ripped through him as the refrigerator wobbled violently, both doors swinging in protest.

"Ahh!" Alex shrieked. Glittering sparks blinded him just before the kitchen vanished into a black abyss. As the carton hit the floor, juice fanned out in shimmering streaks across the linoleum.

* * *

The hospital's noise swelled into a chaotic blur, loudspeakers blaring over frantic voices. Nausea twisted in his gut as fluorescent lights flickered overhead, vanishing into streaks as the gurney sped forward. Disoriented, Alex shut his eyes against the pulsing brightness. After a sharp left turn, the world lurched sideways, slamming into the sharp bite of lingering disinfectant. Urgent voices swarmed around him, but the world was already slipping away.

"Young man, can you hear me?" the doctor asked.

Alex struggled to open his eyes. Words felt thick in his throat, each letter clinging to his tonsils, blocking his speech and fogging his mind. Someone opened the basement door and shone a light down into the dank cavern, waving it around in search of the lost boy.

His mind screamed at the penlight.

Yes, I'm here!

The doctor diagnosed Alex with a closed-head injury and placed him on observation for acute symptoms: vomiting, incoherent speech, headache, dizziness, and confusion. A head X-ray revealed no internal bleeding, nor did it detect the slight swelling in the brain compressing the nervous system.

"A concussion usually requires seven to ten days to heal. We see this all the time. Ramming your head into the freezer door is more common than you think. We'll stanch the bleeding and monitor your son until I authorize his release," the doctor explained, her posture still sharp after hours on her feet.

Hunter Blackwell consoled his wife with a gentle pat on the shoulder. His lips pressed thin, the lines on his forehead etched deep with concern.

"Are there any other tests you can do?" he asked, clearing his throat. "You know, something besides an X-ray?"

"There was a recent publication about a new three-dimensional X-ray machine that uses computed axial tomography. It would give us a better view, but it's still several months away from general use." The doctor shifted her feet, certain this was not what Mr. Blackwell wanted to hear. "Our staff is committed to your son's care," she said, sliding her right hand into her coat pocket to fidget with her pen. "Alex will need plenty of bed rest for a few days. I'll prescribe medication to help with nausea and headaches, if needed. Your son should be up and running in a few days."

✳ ✳ ✳

Back home in the comfort of his room, Alex avoided the grinning cat clock with its glossy black finish. Every tick, every twitch of tail and eyes in unison made the room spin. As the days passed, he progressed to walking without assistance and forming coherent sentences, much to his mother's relief. By the fourth day, he had returned to his old routine of waking at pitch-black o'clock, a habit he'd picked up from his father. "Early to rise makes for significant changes and a productive man," his father always said. "It develops the mind and soul, giving you an edge over everyone else." Alex took all his father's advice to heart, down to his love for fashion and a well-groomed appearance.

The lid on the styling gel opened with a soft pop. Alex inhaled the scent before dipping two fingers into the jar. Rubbing the gel between his palms, he smoothed his hands over his head and worked his fingers through his thick, jet-black hair.

Alex winced when his fingernail scraped his head wound, releasing a new flood. A sharp, rhythmic throb pulsed through the wound, flaring when he glanced into the light. He felt as though his heart would burst out of his head. Short, deep breaths escaped him as he tried to hold back the tears.

Instantly, chemicals seeped into the gash and spread beneath the skin, weaving into his blood-stream. The blue gel contained triethanolamine, which interacted with his brain cells, making them more receptive to external stimuli. His skin prickled as if lightning danced beneath it, and his thoughts scattered like ash in a windstorm. A second compound, iodopropynyl butylcarbamate, intensified the effects. They triggered an unorthodox transformation; electrons rearranged, molecules formed cells, and radical bridges sparked across billions of nerve endings—his body no longer his own, but something newly wired.

That night, a fever took hold, ravaging his already fragile state. Melissa stayed by his side, applying wet towels to his forehead and constantly changing the sweat-drenched bedsheets.

* * *

Several days later, Alex recovered and resumed his daily squabbles with his brother, Bart. He returned to his after-school job at Jonathan Gerstein's minimart. Old man Gerstein was pleasant and cheerful, unlike most of the grumpy men his father associated with in Massapequa. *Living in cold weather most of your life is enough to make anyone grumpy,* was his father's axiom. With his sandy blond hair graying at the temples, Jonathan was a great storyteller, prone to stomping the floor at the story's climax. His wild narratives left listeners laughing more at his idiosyncrasies than the tales themselves. Not a day went by without him whistling a tune from his favorite musical, where one dances joyfully through the neighborhood in the rain.

While replenishing the stockroom, Alex heard the bell above the front door chime. Two sets of footsteps—one heavier than the other—entered, followed by a brief, muffled chat and the sound of a closing door. After stacking a few cases against the wall, he was struck by the stillness—the kind of silence he would expect on an evening stroll through a cemetery. When the ancient floor groaned beneath his feet, the hairs on the back of his neck bristled. He listened for chattering or bursts of laughter, but the silence thickened, pressing against his ears until curiosity clawed its way forward.

Alex crept to the register counter as cautiously as a white-tailed deer venturing into a meadow. He scanned the store for the proprietor, but a glance at the convex mirror revealed nothing but empty aisles. Heart pounding, he stepped around the cylindrical comic book rack to check the register. To his dismay, it was open, the bill compartments empty except for a few stray pennies left behind. He bit down on his knuckles, thinking fast. *Something's wrong. Mr. Gerstein would never leave the register open, not even for a second!* Alex had seen movies like this and knew the likely outcome. Someone usually ended up hurt or dead.

"Mr. Gerstein?" he whispered, the hollows under his eyes darkening with fear. Overhead, the ceiling fans' banana-frond blades spun in rhythm with the ominous throb of the refrigerators. He noticed that the welcome sign at the front door had been turned over to read Sorry, We're Closed.

"Mr. Gerstein, are you here?" he whispered again.

Crack!

A sharp pop of gunfire jolted him. His heart raced as he dashed blindly toward the manager's office. Flinging open the door, he saw Mr. Gerstein's body lying in a pool of blood, still twitching beside the wooden desk. The proprietor's mouth gaped, his eyes transfixed in desperation, but Alex's attention snapped to the two men standing over him. One wore a black leather jacket stretched tight over his belly, failing to conceal the revolver in his hand. His partner held a canvas bag, bulging with cash. Behind them, the steel door of the safe stood wide open.

The rotund thief stared. "What the fuck? Louie, I thought you checked the back."

"Get him!" shouted the other.

Alex stumbled as he turned to run. Air rushed past his face as the chubby one lunged for him. Barely out of reach, he seized the comic book rack and hurled it into his path. The crash sent glossy pages skidding across the floor like autumn leaves. Alex glanced back just in time to see the giant fall, then bolted toward the canned food aisle.

Straining to rise, the hefty man grunted, wobbling as comic books slipped beneath him.

"Chenco, you idiot!" cried Louie. Leaping over his fallen comrade, he rushed down the nearest aisle.

Alex's heart was pounding, his lungs on fire. Louie's head bobbed ahead of him in the next aisle, then rounded the turn to cut him off. Dread coiled in his stomach. With Chenco right behind him, escape was impossible. All he could think about was Mr. Gerstein's lifeless, horror-stricken eyes and how he might soon share the same fate.

Praying the rack would hold his weight, he jumped for the second shelf and reached for the aisle's supporting wall. His left foot hit the next shelf, sending a shower of goods careening to the floor. Amid the clattering cans, Alex shrieked at the sudden jolt, but his fingers found the rim. Arms straining, he thrust himself over the supporting wall and swung his feet onto the top shelf. Boxes of cold medicine scattered into the air. *No time to rest!* He rolled off the shelf and landed on all fours, crushing the boxes beneath him.

Purple high-tops screeched to a halt where Alex had been just seconds earlier. Louie's face turned bright red and the veins at his temples throbbed. "Lucky bastard!" he shouted, breathing heavily through his narrow nose and kicking several cans in frustration. The overhead light shadowed his squinting eyes, distorting his face into a dreadful mask.

Chenco, still panting from the chase, managed to grab Alex's left shoe before the boy cleared the aisle. He slammed it against the broken shelf, sending down another cascade of cans.

"Come on!" Louie shoved Chenco aside and led the way into the next aisle, where his sneakers again squeaked to a sudden stop. The boy was gone. Instead, small boxes littered the floor like confetti, crushed from his landing. Inching ahead, Chenco followed the barrel of his gun down the aisle. His brown eyes shone with fierce determination. Since the kid had seen their faces, getting him was imperative. Even if that meant shooting the punk at point-blank range, just like Mr. Gerstein.

Convinced they would find the boy, Louie was already plotting diabolical ways to dispose of the body. He stood quietly by the stockroom, his eyes wild and his bony jaw clamped tight. "Flush him out!" he barked, his eyes squinting into the dimness. He used so few words when he spoke that his sentences were often as short as those in cheap telegrams. After a few tense minutes, Chenco reappeared, empty-handed and puzzled. Louie slammed the wall with his fist. *I'm sick of this game. We should've ended this already!* He gritted his teeth in silent fury and focused on the last remaining door. His chapped lips curled into a snarl.

Perched on the sink, Alex pictured himself dead on the bathroom floor, wide-eyed, blood pooling beneath him. His heart thudded as he fought for air. After a futile tug at the window, he leaped off the sink. Even if he could squeeze through the narrow opening, the rusty security bars would stop him cold. Powerless, he wondered if his death was inevitable. Maybe they'd let him go if he just waved his T-shirt in surrender. *Isn't that how it's done in movies? Or is that only between friends playing cops and robbers?*

Alex panted, knowing he had to keep fighting. He ran into the stall and locked the wooden door, his eyes squeezed shut.

Outside, Louie grinned and rapped on the bathroom door. "Come out, come out, wherever you are."

Annoyed, Chenco pushed him aside and yelled, "That's enough with the fuckin' horseplay. I'll show you how it's done!"

A forceful kick sent the strike plate ripping off the door frame. Chenco drew his gun and stepped into the bathroom, kicking the metal plate with his heavy boot. It scraped across the floor and struck the toilet with a clatter. Startled by the noise, he fired blindly. The bullet tore through the thin partition, whizzed past Alex's head, and pierced the brick wall. Debris sprayed his neck, yet he remained still. His dry mouth tightened, and his aching legs trembled from squatting on the toilet seat cover. There was no shame when the tears welling in his eyes finally spilled over. Had he stayed home today, he'd be running in the park with his dog instead of running for his life. Taking a deep breath, he twisted his torso and placed his trembling hands against the cool brick wall. He shut his eyes tightly, wishing he could be where the birds fly free, bask in the sun's warmth on his bare back, and stand beside his arrogant older brother—though that last thought left a bitter taste.

Suddenly, a wave of tingling sensations washed over him, as if every molecule inside him was being ripped apart like grains of sand tumbling in an hourglass, as though God's massive lungs had blown a mighty blast of air through him. He stifled a scream when his hands and arms disappeared. Then a gust of fresh air whipped through his hair, and before he realized it, his body had rematerialized on the other side of the brick wall. Confused and frightened, Alex huddled in the same position with the sun warming his sweat-drenched back. Examining his body for gashes or oozing blood, he struggled to make sense of his ordeal.

Am I delusional?

He ran home, not even missing the lost shoe, feeling lucky to be alive.

✳ ✳ ✳

Days later, Alex explained his newfound ability— what he called clearing—to his parents and siblings in the garage. He preferred not to use the word disappear; clearing involved erasing all thoughts except for the location where he wanted to rematerialize.

"Dream on," said Bart with a snigger. "Now that you have all of us together, are you going to lay a gasser?"

Elizabeth and Walter laughed.

Melissa looked at her husband, who leaned forward in response to her pleading eyes and said, "Be cool, guys."

Bart sighed heavily and rolled his eyes. "Dad, you know he's only trying to psych us out!" he said, stomping his foot.

"Nevertheless, let's give him our undivided attention," his father said, one brow raised in warning.

Bart challenged his younger brother, hoping to turn the tables. "Why don't you 'clear' into that empty freezer before I dip out, you spaz?" he sneered, his nose creasing.

Determined to put his brother in his place, Alex cleared his mind and concentrated on the vacant space inside the chest freezer. He pictured himself inside, snickering at their stunned expressions. Ignoring the junk accumulated on the hinged lid, he stared intensely at the freezer. Liz erupted into giggles at his contorted face, her braces glinting in the harsh overhead light cradled in cobwebs. Then, pressing her hands to her mouth, she watched her brother concentrate, anticipation flickering in her eyes.

Suddenly, he was gone. Vanished. Liz, Bart, and Walt stood agape. Stunned, no one, especially not Bart, dared move a muscle. Then Liz screamed, "Far out!"

The avocado-green freezer sat askew against the wall, secured with a padlock to prevent the children from getting trapped inside and suffocating. Despite the distractions, Alex had successfully teleported into the freezer. The stale air weighed on his lungs. Even worse, he hadn't counted on the small space triggering awful memories of his trauma in the bathroom stall. In the pitch black, he shut his eyes and focused on the cool garage floor just outside. After several tense seconds, he opened his eyes. He thought Bart had turned off the garage light, but his head bumped against the lid when he leaned forward. Realizing he was still confined, he concentrated even harder on the garage floor, but still nothing happened.

Now panicked, he bellowed for help, fists hammering the walls.

"Somebody *please* do something!" Melissa pleaded hysterically, but no one knew where the padlock key was kept. Alex's faint screams continued, and the more he cried for help, the more distressed his mother became.

"Out of the way!" Hunter shouted, charging toward the freezer with an ax hoisted over his shoulder. He swept aside the accumulated junk on the lid and swung at the padlock with such ferocity that everyone recoiled as the ax struck the lock with a sharp clang. Sparks flew on the sixth attempt, and the padlock burst open. With the pop of suction releasing, Alex heaved the lid up and leaped out, his burning lungs gasping for air, his thin arms flailing.

After a few supervised experiments, Hunter determined that his son's ability to clear only worked in the presence of light, either natural or artificial. He explained that life is dependent on light. "It says so in the Bible," he boasted. "Genesis 1:3: 'And God said, "Let there be light!"' From then on, life took form: plants, trees, and living creatures." He stressed that Alex should never attempt to clear in total darkness, a precept not to be taken lightly.

Hunter didn't know how his son acquired this ability to vanish and rematerialize, and he preferred it to remain a mystery. He was certain that revealing the secret would bring relentless media scrutiny. Their life as a close-knit family would end. The thought of jeopardizing precious family time sent shivers down his spine. *The kids would love that*, he thought, his aging blue eyes darkening with despair. Worse, their private affairs would be splashed across every television show and tabloid nationwide. Reporters would embellish Alex's story with idiotic headlines like Disappearing Boy Visits Earth from Faraway Galaxy! Dodging hundreds, possibly thousands, of people vying for prized snapshots with their zoom lens cameras was not the life he wanted for his wife and four children: Alexander, the gifted one; Bartholomew, the proud one; Elizabeth, the sweet one; and Walter, the quiet one.

Never revealing Alex's secret became the new family rule. Though it pained his heart, Hunter ensured compliance by periodically lecturing his son on safety and prohibiting him from playing with the neighborhood kids.

Despite his father's best efforts to instill a moral center, Alex chose the path of corruption. His appetite was avaricious, and no amount of seasoning could alter his taste for wealth. He soon discovered that objects could clear with him, provided none carried an electrical current. Without considering the consequences, clearing stolen goods became a daily habit. After a few weeks of perfecting his skills, he craved bigger risks—first cleaning out cash registers in neighborhood stores, then moving on to more valuable prizes. It took several years before he thought to carry a 3-liter canister of oxygen if things went wrong.

By age thirty-two, Alex focused exclusively on high-end jewelry stores, seeking gold bracelets, ropes of pearls, and diamond earrings. Clearing gave him power beyond anything he'd ever known. He funded a lavish lifestyle for years by selling premium articles to a loyal out-of-state broker. His biggest haul: two sacks of Russian diamonds, lifted from an international distributor and sold to a famous retail chain specializing in engagement rings. The sale included the declaration, Kimberley certificate, and altered origin and ownership paperwork.

Alex closed the deal at the buyer's bank, offering exclusive watches to James Jaramillo and his associate, Donald Kennings, thereby securing their confidence. Back at the office, James settled comfortably in his chair, his face riddled with wrinkles that resembled dried-out, cracked mud. When others spoke, he often pressed his index finger over his upper lip. Alex couldn't help thinking he looked like the kind of guy who would loudly suck on a wooden toothpick at dinner.

Beside him, Donald's thin lips gave him a serpent-like impression when he smiled. He knew everything about raw-cut diamonds and was well aware these had been stolen. Still, the considerable savings were enough for him to overlook the fraud. A smirk formed on his lips: curling with the sly unease of an Eastern garter snake. *Who gives a fuck where he got them? The company's already ahead of the game, so I'm fine with it.*

Men like James and Donald were fixtures in Alex's world—where charm was just lacquer over rot, and every handshake came with a whisper.

Later that week, Alex slipped into a different role—this time for his father. Though unemployed, he claimed to be managing a high-profile corporation in Manhattan. "You should see the office," he said smugly. "From the thirty-sixth floor, I can see the baseball fields in Central Park."

"Bet you can see every game on a clear day," his father said, giving his son's shoulder a congratulatory pat.

Alex's ego swelled at the pride in his father's eyes. If he played his cards right, he could go on forever. He pushed aside the curtain and gazed out into his father's yard. "Sometimes I can hear the crack of the bat on a home run," he said, and they both burst out laughing.

Alex spent his days casing stores in Wantagh, Seaford, Amityville, Oyster Bay, and Massapequa for valuables he could turn over for quick profit. Clearing into bank vaults was easier than drilling holes into the lockboxes, using mirrors to study the lock's wheels, or messing with nitroglycerin to blow the vault door. "Eat your heart out, John Dillinger!" he would cry when clearing from a vault.

Still, he faced problems, particularly with determining the safest altitude for materializing. With a miscalculation, he might reappear anywhere from three inches to three feet above the floor, sending him tumbling. A few bruises were nothing. His arrogance and neglect did the real damage.

* * *

Thursday, March 18, 2004.

The day after the incident with the fuel tanker, Alex decided to deposit his ID and credit cards in a bus depot locker. Eventually, he recognized the need for a lookout and picked his girlfriend, Stacey Foster, as the perfect accomplice. To his chagrin, his request astounded her. She could not fathom how a man with such an extraordinary gift could think only of corrupt ends.

"This God-given power should be used for the good of the people. You should be saving lives and helping police apprehend criminals!" she argued, her body planted firmly in front of him. "Find a way to save our world from corruption instead of adding to it." But her pleas meant nothing. When he shrugged off her concerns, she rolled her eyes and stalked out in a huff.

Stacey wanted nothing to do with his power. She insisted she wasn't interested in money, a claim supported by her wealthy background. Despite the tension, she knew she could always rely on her mother, Kathryn, for a quick loan in a crisis. As a registered nurse, she earned enough to support her lifestyle.

Two years after Stacey's father, Bradley, passed away, doubts lingered about the circumstances of his death. Though she hated to admit it, Stacey suspected her mother of killing him to control the $85 million empire.

Worsening the betrayal, her brother, Erik, seven years her senior, had been pushed out of the family pharmaceutical business after a bitter dispute with their power-hungry mother. As CEO, Kathryn stripped her son of his lucrative executive role. The board of directors saw it as a family disgrace, but they said nothing, relieved it was him, not one of them.

Erik cut all ties with their rapacious mother, refusing to speak to her again. But Stacey couldn't afford to ignore Kathryn. Not yet. If she wanted answers about her father's death, she had to dig deeper.

* * *

During successive visits to her mother's house, Stacey secretly installed and retrieved an apparatus between the keyboard and computer to record keystrokes, letting her retrieve stored data without loss. Wearing a pink robe and a towel wrapped around her head, she pulled the floral curtains aside, letting the sun's warmth fill her room. Two lamps centered on a royal-blue accent wall highlighted the landscape oil painting. An elegant chess storage box with gold and silver pieces rested on a wooden lift-top coffee table. Stacey and Alex had spent countless hours locked in strategic battle, though he could only claim victory in one of their many games.

Settling into her desk chair, Stacey installed the keystroke device and booted up her computer without disturbing the towel on her damp hair. Her gaze settled on a photo of her and Alex at a local ice-skating rink, and she quickly looked away. Despite her feelings for him, she wasn't sure she could accept his criminal tendencies. Until she sorted through those tangled emotions, seeing him again would come with its challenges. Blinking away the tears, Stacey set her jaw and activated the device, downloading her mother's keystrokes.

* * *

With Kathryn away for the long Independence Day weekend, Stacey took an extra vacation day to search for evidence about her father's death. After easily hacking into Kathryn's computer, she pecked at the keyboard with her manicured fingers. Shock morphed into revulsion, then anger as she scrolled through business documents that detailed the firing of four board members and a 10 percent reduction in the workforce. Her father would have been livid. Then she paused over a cryptic entry in Kathryn's daily planner:

May 23, 2002, 1:35 a.m.

The Spanish software was successfully installed.

Strange. Especially considering her hatred of Spanish. How could she have installed a program the night dad passed away? Clicking more slowly, she found an entry mentioning a dust-like substance. A quick search brought up a page describing Spanphyx in disturbing detail. Stacey grimaced. The name's resemblance to *Spanish* couldn't be a coincidence.

Stacey learned that the powder, typically sold on the Asian black market, caused suffocation. She read aloud: "In a moist environment, the microscopic particles expand to one thousand times their original size. If inhaled, they cause death by asphyxiation."

"Oh!" Stacey cried, then hit print.

* * *

After successfully clearing into the jewelry store, Alex stood before a U-shaped counter, its glass surface veiled by a pristine white sheet that hid a cache of riches. On the wall, mirrored displays held opulent necklaces, glimmering under the security lights like constellations in the desert sky. Silent as a shadow, Alex scowled beneath his ski mask, defying the watchful cameras as he whisked the sheets away to reveal the coveted jewels. Mindful of the ticking clock and the threat of silent alarms, he withdrew a ball-peen hammer from the pouch at his waist and shattered the glass in swift, surgical strikes. Ornate watches, gleaming diamond rings, and shimmering pearl necklaces were each in turn tucked carefully into the pouch.

The sound of a low growl made him freeze in mid-grab.

A glance over his shoulder confirmed his fear. A pair of gleaming eyes fixed on him, above a row of wicked teeth. Before he could blink, the black Rottweiler lunged. Alex flung himself over the counter just as powerful jaws clamped onto the heel of his left shoe, ripping it off his foot. As he sailed over the shattered glass, he sliced his hand on a jagged shard before plunging down the far side. With a menacing growl, the Rottweiler dropped the shoe and pounced after him.

Alex's body slammed onto the floor with a sickening thud, knocking the wind out of him. He had to clear out before the police arrived. *I must get the coordinates to clear!* Breathing in painful gasps, he forced himself to all fours and started to stand up, but the Rottweiler's weight flung him to his back.

Teeth bared, the Rottweiler loomed over him.

Alex flailed, trying to keep it at bay, flinching as drooling jaws snapped shut. A flurry of punches landed, but the dog barely flinched. The beast lunged again, claws raking his chest. Holding the dog's neck with his left hand, he shielded his face with the other.

Then he saw it coming.

The bite caught flesh first, then only air. He pulled his hand back just in time.

His knee struck a forceful blow to its belly. *Yelp!* Bloodied but free, Alex scrambled to his feet and drove a series of kicks to its groin until it lay motionless.

Sweat clung beneath the mask, stinging his eyes as his lungs burned with every wheeze. The wail of sirens assaulted his ears. Leaping back over the counter, he reached for his mangled shoe just as a police car screeched to a halt in front of the jewelry store. The dispatcher's voice crackled through the two-way radio, like static tearing through a storm. Without hesitation, Alex snatched up the jewelry pouch, fixed his eyes across the intersection, and cleared, leaving the shoe behind.

The serene night sky glittered with stars and the moon shone through the low clouds, casting a soft glow over the landscape below. Rematerializing next to his parked car, Alex gingerly climbed in wearing only one shoe and pulled off his ski mask. For a fleeting moment, he watched the swarm of police cars converge before pulling away. The night's haul would have to wait until he dressed his wounds.

* * *

Stacey parked behind the others in the circular driveway of her mother's two-story colonial home. With a passing look, she noticed the perennial flowers on the island hadn't returned, but the burning bush and liriope, nestled around the lampposts, were thriving. Alex stood in front of the graceful steps, waiting. As she approached, she took a deep breath, unsure whether calling him had been the right choice. Yet the way he moved with such ease, paired with that enchanting smile, brought her a sense of comfort and led her to clasp his hand.

She gasped, pulling his hand closer to inspect it. "How on earth did this happen?"

"It's nothing to worry about." He dismissed her concern blithely. "I cut myself on some broken glass."

"Alex, I see the cuts from the glass, but these," she ran her finger over the still-raw gashes, "these are puncture wounds. Either a snake or a dog did this."

He waved off her concern. "It's fine. I've cleaned and disinfected them thoroughly, but if you insist, I promise to see a doctor first thing tomorrow morning." His uninjured hand gave a cocky three-fingered salute.

Stacey's eyes narrowed. Something about his tone didn't sit right, but here and now wasn't the place to press him, so she let it go.

He offered his elbow with exaggerated charm and said, "Now, let's go meet your mother."

They entered the reception hall, where the polished marble floors gleamed under the chandelier's soft light. Alex was captivated by the foyer, particularly its Renaissance-style domed ceiling. A quiet presence approached to take their coats. She was a tall woman with a hawk-like nose and shoulders as rigid as a wooden clothes hanger, her thin-framed glasses perched precariously on the bridge.

"When you said your family was well off, you didn't mention they were filthy rich," he remarked as Stacey led him under the imperial staircase toward the gathering room, his eyes on the sway of her hips.

"I don't like to talk about my parents, especially not since my father passed away two years ago. This was his empire. Unfortunately, my mother and I have . . . drifted apart since the funeral," she said carefully.

Stacey pushed open the glass doors, revealing an exquisite Goertz grand piano and an eight-piece ensemble performing Tchaikovsky's *Variations on a Rococo Theme,* based on Fitzenhagen's arrangement. The cellist's eyes were closed as his fingers danced effortlessly across the fingerboard. His body swayed in time to the music, mirroring the strings' emotional resonance.

Impressive, thought Alex.

The limestone walls radiated warmth, reflecting off the black marble flooring. Olive-green sofas sat slightly askew, accompanied by a bronze sculpture of a naked man sitting in quiet contemplation atop a black marble end table. Behind the ensemble, a sleek glass wall framed a panoramic view of a

Japanese garden, complete with a koi pond framed by cherry and bonsai trees.

Kathryn had never appreciated this style. It had been her husband's vision for the gathering room, which he had enjoyed for several years. If it were up to her, she would recreate an early 1800s European salon, featuring French Empire-style furniture, a Georgian armoire, and long drapes in shades of morel-mushroom brown, palm-leaf green, and island-sand beige.

"Stacey, my dear," Kathryn said, extending her arms and gliding across the floor with spurious affection and a gleam in her eye for Stacey's handsome companion. Her ostentatious display of rings and bracelets dimmed against the necklace draped above her plunging neckline—a single 18-carat Colombian emerald, its rich spruce green encased in a sunburst of diamonds. Each facet caught the light with mesmerizing fire.

The two women leaned forward, lips puckered, and exchanged successive air kisses. "This is Alex," Stacey said, her smile wavering as her mother's eyes lingered on him. "I told you about him a while back, remember?"

"I can't remember what I did yesterday, Stacey. How do you expect me to keep track of *all* your boyfriends? You change them like your underwear." She sounded a little tipsy. "You *do* wear underwear, don't you, dear?"

Alex took her outstretched hand, cupping it in his, and kissed the spot just above her knuckles to break the tension. His gaze lingered on the glittering rock on her right middle finger, quietly estimating its worth. He straightened, meeting her piercing gaze, making him feel both vulnerable and captivated. Her gaze brimmed with desire, yet left no room for submission. She was in control, and no man would ever take that away from her. Her short, sandy hair and radiant skin dazzled under the ambient light. His body responded to her touch as he imagined the feel of her geranium-pink lips and the firm curves accentuated by her dress.

A smirk spread across Kathryn's face as she assessed him, admiring his square jaw and full lips. The warm lighting cast soft shadows on his brows, deepening the mesmerizing blue of his eyes. His sharp taste in clothes emphasized broad shoulders and a ramrod-straight posture, the embodiment of quiet confidence. For a fleeting moment, she imagined him hovering ecstatically over her trembling form, reveling in the touch of her smooth skin. With a confidence born of her own desirability, Kathryn slid her arm through his and led him away, eager to display him to the guests.

Stacey expected this behavior from her mother, but that didn't make it easier to accept. It was why she'd distanced herself . . . yet she always came back for more. Ever since Kathryn had expunged Erik from the family trust, Stacey had endured her mother's mistreatment in hopes of helping him regain his rightful control.

Her loyalty to Erik ran deep, shaped by moments long before trust funds and betrayals. She remembered one moment vividly—grammar school, and a girl named Antoinette Stoltzfus. Plump, with medium-length strawberry blonde hair and bulging brown eyes, Antoinette looked as if she were hoarding mothballs in her cheeks. She fancied herself both brilliant and tough, crediting books for her brains and baseball for her right hook. Socially, she was a disaster.

"I don't like how you comb your stupid hair," Antoinette sneered at Erik, her gelatinous cheeks jiggling with each poke into his skinny chest.

Stacey rushed over before Antoinette could lay another hand on him. She stepped in front of Erik, crossed her arms, and declared, "I'm tired of you bullying other kids, Antoinette!"

"So-o-o?" Antoinette drawled, expelling her foul breath with every syllable. A cluster of boys appeared, anticipating a scuffle, or better yet a full-on catfight. Antoinette placed her hands on her hips, challenging Stacey with a raised brow. "And just what are you going to do about—"

Stacey's fist collided with Antoinette's soft, chubby cheek, sending her plummeting into the two boys behind her while the other three stood, mouths agape. After that, neither Erik nor Stacey ever heard from Antoinette again.

"You strike me as a man who knows exactly what he wants," Kathryn purred, stopping next to her full-size replica of Michelangelo's *David*. The statue, made of white resin, stood brazenly beside the bar, gathering strength before facing Goliath. At the other end of the bar stood a copy of Donatello's version of David, graceful and relaxed after his monumental battle.

Alex ordered a drink, surreptitiously glancing at David's genitalia, measuring up, grateful he wasn't born in the same era. "Depends what I'm after," he said with a grin, raising the glass to his lips. He could feel Kathryn's calculating stare, stripping away the layers of his confidence with quiet precision. There was no need for games here. He wanted her just as much as she wanted him.

Stacey chatted with her grandfather, whose short white hair resembled a cockatoo's ruffled feathers. Bushy brows leaped out from his round, red face, and the corners of his eyes drooped. His mouth popped open whenever he looked up, giving him a constant air of surprise. In between their stilted comments, Stacey stole glances at Alex, still intensely focused on her mother. Even from across the room, she could see the glimmer of amusement and lust in her lover's eyes. Shifting uncomfortably in her seat, Grandpa Fred rambled on about overcoming alcoholism, his words falling on deaf ears while she nodded along politely.

"I woke up in the park, not knowing where I was or even who I was," said Fred, his mind trailing off. Then he resumed, tapping her shoulder. "That was when I realized I needed help. And look at me now!" He hopped up joyfully, maintaining his balance as Stacey reached out to steady him with a laugh.

"Yes, I can see you've been saved, Grandpa." To her relief, Fred excused himself to use the bathroom. Smiling, she watched him shuffle lightly across the almost liquid floor, which only seemed to increase his desire to urinate. As Stacey turned to reclaim Alex, an older woman with wrinkled, insistent fingers tugged at her sleeve. Though her movements were slow and deliberate, she muttered something about the ensemble's final and most challenging variation, an allegro vivo.

"Do you like classical music, my dear?" the woman asked, her voice tinged with nervous eagerness to connect.

Stacey shot her a glare, her patience worn thin. *This is a nightmare. Why must I deal with all these annoying people?* Rolling her eyes, she said, "Actually, I'm into rap."

Startled, the woman nearly spit out her champagne, but Stacey was already walking away.

* * *

Over the next few months, Stacey noticed a shift in Alex's behavior. Subtle changes, yet obvious to someone in love. Weak excuses replaced intimacy. Promises crumbled as romantic dinners became hurried fast-food stops, mere conveniences for his so-called evening obligations. At 4:35 one morning, he pulled up in front of Stacey's house after spending the night with Kathryn. With the engine and heater running, he stripped off his clothes, stuffed them into a drawstring sack, and shoved it beneath the driver's seat. Ripping open a packet of unscented moist towelettes, he dragged one briskly over his body to erase any trace of Kathryn. Then he slipped into a spandex T-shirt, wool pants, and leather moccasins designed to minimize friction and noise.

Having mastered stealth over his years of burglarizing homes and stores, Alex stood quietly on the terrace. Flexing his feet, he popped his ankles—ensuring they wouldn't crack as he crept through the house. Slowly, he inserted the key and turned the handle to retract the latch before exerting pressure on the door. A slight upward tug kept the hinges from squeaking as he slipped through the narrow opening. Pushing the door against the frame, the bolt quietly slid into place. With slow, measured breaths, he stayed near the walls, where the wooden floors had less play, and avoided shifting his weight until his lead foot was firmly planted. When he reached Stacey's bedside, he stood listening for several minutes before surreptitiously easing into bed.

She feigned sleep, her silent tears soaking into her pillowcase.

* * *

Stacey didn't need a fortune teller; she already suspected Alex had been sleeping with her mother from the beginning. Even so, she needed to see it for herself. One windy evening, she followed his car east on Sunrise Highway but lost sight of him when he turned right onto Farmingdale Road. She scanned the streets for any sign of him. Just as he turned onto Main Street, she caught sight of his car again and tailed it to the Travelin' Horseman Restaurant.

Brittle maple leaves swarmed across the intersection, pitter-pattering like hundreds of hermit crabs scrambling across a sunbaked pier. Three bicyclists sliced through the cascade while the wind whipped up the fabric of one rider's unbuttoned shirt, streaming behind him like a ribbon of melted chocolate.

Bundled up in a beige fur coat and matching hat, Stacey's mother stood by the entrance, cigarette in hand. Alex stepped out of his car, draped in the black leather trench coat Stacey had given him for his birthday. She burned with rage, remembering the hours spent locating the style he'd seen in a magazine. And now he was showing it off to another woman—her mother, no less!—flashing that bemused smile as if nothing were wrong. He even had the audacity to kiss Kathryn in public. Stacey's lips tingled as she wondered whether her mother felt that same electric thrill. Casually, Alex slipped his arm around Kathryn. The low hum of live jazz spilled into the night as he pulled open the door, and they disappeared inside.

Stacey had promised herself she would never shed tears for any man, especially those who cared only about their egos, but she was so overcome with rage that breaking down was therapeutic. She pulled out sharply from the curb and cut off a young man, who missed clipping her car by inches.

"Hey, bitch! Watch where you're fuckin' going," the other driver shouted, adding a rude gesture and a few choice insults about female drivers. But his cries were in vain, for Stacey had already vanished.

* * *

Three days later, on a Sunday afternoon, Stacey paid her mother an unannounced visit, primed for a woman-to-woman talk. She took a deep breath and looked her mother square in the eyes. "I know about you and Alex, Mother."

Kathryn sipped her tequila, savoring the burn as it slid down her throat. "I was starting to wonder if you had the balls to confront me." She set the glass on the end table beside the grand piano and walked to the bar where her designer bag lay. With practiced ease, she dug through the depths for a cigarette and lighter. Before the flame lit, the glass whizzed past her head and shattered against the wall, staining the limestone with tequila and barely missing a 10-foot abstract wall sculpture. Kathryn looked at the broken glass serenely. "My, you really *do* have balls."

"Now you listen to me, mother dear," Stacey said, getting in her face. "You have no idea what you're getting yourself into. Alex is dangerous! I'd advise you to stay clear of him."

Kathryn lit her cigarette, took a drag, and blew

the smoke into her face. "You know what your problem is, Stacey," she said with a twitch of her nose. "You don't know how to hold on to a man. You never have."

Stacey struggled to control her anger, her jaw clenched, a vein bulging at her temple. "I know all about how you ensnare your men. I'm ashamed to be the daughter of a slut like you!"

The slap came fast and hard, leaving a burning red mark. Stacey squeezed her eyes shut as pain shot down her spine. In disbelief, she brought a trembling hand to her throbbing face. "Don't you *dare* lay a finger on me ever again, or so help me—"

"What do you intend to do, Stacey?" asked Kathryn, inching closer. "Cry like the little pathetic girl you—"

Stacey's fist smashed into her mother's startled face, sending her tumbling backward into *David*. The imitation hit the floor with a sharp clatter and sent shards skittering across the hard surface. Dazed, Kathryn sat up and felt her bloodied lip, then reached with an unsteady hand to pick up a broken piece. Her features twisted as she realized the piece was David's scrotum and shriveled-up penis. Embarrassed, she tossed it back into the pile.

Kathryn stood up, teetering on her stilettos, and shrieked, "Get out of my house!" Her hair was in disarray, and her bloodshot eyes bulged with fury. Tension twisted her face. "First thing Monday morning, I'm writing you out of the will! Do you hear me? Just like your pathetic brother. You'll never have any of this! And you'll never lay a hand on my jewelry!"

"Don't worry, Mother. I'll make sure you're buried with your jewels."

Stacey left without another word.

"You are out, I tell you!" Kathryn's final battle cry rang out, a lock of hair straggling over her left eye.

* * *

A single cell vibrated into existence, followed by trillions more. If slowed to a crawl, they could be seen agitating the air as they bonded into intricate patterns. Yet in a fraction of a second, Alex materialized, dressed in his tight-fitting all-black outfit and ski mask.

Silence hung in the air like a woolen blanket. The men's department store was empty, but Alex was used to the eerie stillness. He moved quietly down the aisle, passing neatly stacked dress shirts on wall shelves and carefully arranged sweaters on display tables. Mannequins showcased expensive suits in calculated poses.

Alex picked up the calf-length burgundy coat with blue-and-gold paisley lining he'd been eyeing for a few days. Standing before a large mirror, he tried the coat on even though he'd already done so while casing the place. The coat gave him an air of finesse, and he knew the color alone would set him apart from the black or gray most men typically wore.

"I must say, that is one very stylish coat," a thin, breathy voice said from behind.

Alex spun around, his eyes widening and his heart shifting into second gear.

An older man with prominent rosacea smiled up at him. Bone degeneration had humped his spine, and his arms were covered in intricate Navy tattoos.

Untidy snow-white hair reminded Alex of a cockatoo's ruffled feathers.

"Didn't mean to startle you," the man said with a chuckle as he stepped up to smooth out the shoulder pad. "Quite dapper indeed."

The man didn't seem threatening, so Alex's heart shifted back to first. Still, he remained alert.

The stranger's eyes narrowed. Concentrating, he cocked his head to one side and said, "I've seen you before." He placed a forefinger to his lips to breathe life into his elusive memory. "Can't remember where, but I recognize those eyes. I never forget eyes, my friend."

Alex shifted his gaze to avoid further scrutiny. "I've never seen you before in my life."

"From afar," replied the man, nodding. He leaned closer, showering Alex with his hot breath and locking eyes in a moment of shared understanding. "Like two ships passing in the night." He turned to walk away, assuming the stranger would follow. "How did you get in here anyway?" he asked in a raspy voice.

"I have my ways," replied Alex, keeping pace

behind him.

"That's quite all right. You don't have to tell me," the man said. "I don't stick my nose in other people's business." Stopping next to a square pillar, he stooped to retrieve a brown paper bag and slid into a sitting position. "Come, sit down." He flexed his fingers twice, the joints cracking. "Have a drink with me."

"Thanks, but I must be going."

"You don't know what you're missing. Look," said the man, pulling down the brown bag to reveal a bottle of high-end whiskey.

Alex raised an eyebrow at the label. Definitely not the kind of bottle you'd find in a paper bag. "On second thought, I suppose I can spare a few more minutes."

With a chortle, the man said, "I knew you could be bought." He untwisted the cap, handed Alex a glass, and poured out a generous measure of liquid gold. They clinked the bottle and glass together. The old man wriggled against the post with a contented sigh and said, "My youth adventurer ID says my name is Fred."

"Nice to make your acquaintance, Fred." Alex held out his hand. With no intention of removing his mask, he said, "My name is . . . Misterio." They shared a laugh. As the whiskey flowed down his throat, Alex closed his eyes, savoring the warmth that spread through him. "If you don't mind me asking, how did *you* get in here?"

"I'm an adventurer!" said Fred, raising his bottle to toast his achievement.

"That's a funny way of saying homeless."

The man laughed heartily. "Young man, I'm far from homeless. And it's true, I *am* an adventurer."

"Pray tell."

Fred smiled, reminiscing. "I've always wondered what it would be like to stow away on a pirate ship. To sail the deep blue seas in search of monsters and sirens that sing enchanting songs from rocky shores. To be caught up in a sea battle with cannons blazing, the mast shivering, a pirate banner snapping overhead." He leaned forward, wielding an imaginary sword between his arthritic fingers. "This is the last time you and your crew will sail the West

African seas, Duque de Misterio!" he shouted, waving Alex into the scene.

Picking up on his cue, Alex crawled forward and faced the one-eyed scourge of the great Atlantic.

"You will pillage and kill no more, Captain Frederick!" the Duque de Misterio shouted, ordering his fervent crew to fire the cannons. Plumes of smoke billowed into the air, obscuring the once-clear sky as a cannonball pierced the ship's wooden hull.

Many projectiles splashed into the sea, spattering frigid waters over the wooden deck. Captain Frederick stood his ground fearlessly, wishing he could make the Duque eat his words as a main course in the mess hall. He pointed his sword at the Duque. "Swing 'er round and fire!" he ordered his crew of bloodthirsty savages. Cannonballs bombarded the ship. One struck the mast and splintered it into toothpicks, sending sailors scrambling. Another hit the hull with a boom, spraying debris across the deck. The Duque's ship lay in ruins, engulfed in flames and sinking into the ocean's depths.

"You haven't heard the last of me, Captain Frederick!" shouted the Duque de Misterio. "Mark my words. I'll defeat you if it's the last thing I do! Full sail ahead!"

Fred sat back, confused. "Did you just say 'Full sail ahead'?"

"Ah, yeah."

"You do know you're sinking, right?"

Laughing at his own ignorance, Alex returned to the pillar and sat beside Fred, whose hysterical guffaws shook his body.

When they finally calmed down, Fred took another swig from the bottle. "As a child, I wondered what it would be like to do anything. Now, I do everything I once dreamed of. Since I can't stow away on a pirate ship, I stow away in department stores. Sometimes I hide in the bathroom with my feet up on the toilet seat and wait for the store to close. Once the coast is clear, I wander around, trying on whatever catches my eye. I enjoy this newfound freedom and the adventures I conjure up in my crafty little head." Swirling the whiskey around in the bottle, he took a long, slow whiff and allowed the aroma to ferment in his brain. Then he asked, "Have you ever been in jail?"

"Never," replied Alex, "Nor do I plan to."

"I've been thrown into the slammer twenty-seven times," Fred admitted.

"You're shitting me."

"I shit you not," Fred replied with a smirk. "I've been in jail so many times, the police chief shakes his head whenever he sees me. He knows my kids' phone numbers by heart. Within an hour or two, I'm back home . . . right where I *don't* want to be." He gazed at Alex, who stared back, processing his words. "I run in the rain and splash in the puddles naked because that's what I want to do. Daring things no one considers doing in a zillion years." He turned and looked Alex squarely in the eyes. "Have you ever gone skydiving?"

"Can't say that I have."

"It's exhilarating! The wind wraps around you, pulling you down and in seconds, you're plummeting toward the Earth at a terminal velocity of a hundred and twenty miles an hour!" Fred exclaimed. He extended his arms, rocking back and forth as if gliding through turbulent winds. His right hand brushed against Alex's face, forcing him to look away. Then, he batted his eyelids, puffed out his cheeks, and swished the air side to side to simulate free fall. Turning to Alex, he shouted, "You ought to try this! It's like a forty-four-hundred-watt hairdryer blowing in your face, whipping up your locks to slap your handsome features a trillion times!"

Alex's eyes sparkled as he doubled over with laughter. Hopping to his feet, he said, "You mean like this!" Alex crouched and extended his arms, flapping them against the rushing air. His face contorted as he puffed out his cheeks and batted his eyes to avoid the strong current. "Oh no!" he shouted, looking over his shoulder. "I forgot my parachute!"

They ended the skydive with a hearty round of laughter. Fred's eccentricity captured Alex's imagination. He sat back down and leaned into Fred's shoulder, laughing until his muscles ached. Eventually, they subsided into a soft chuckle and a sigh of relief.

Later, Fred stood with great care, mindful not to wake the joint pains that had gone into hibernation.

"Where are you going?" asked Alex, surprised.

"I gotta tinkle. Back in a flash, scrotum rash." Fred walked away gingerly to avoid releasing the floodgates.

Alex nodded with amusement. "Great, now I have a new name."

Pouring himself another glass of whiskey, Alex reflected on his life. Just a few days ago, he was in the powerful jaws of a Rottweiler, fearing for his life and desperately fighting for the upper hand, a violent struggle that felt endless. And today he was enjoying drinks with a stranger and listening to his charming tales. He lifted the glass to his lips, but before he could take another sip, he heard Fred hollering. Fearing for his new friend's safety, he jumped up and ran to the aisle, his heart pounding with alarm.

"What the fuck," said Alex. His eyes widened as the old-timer ran down the aisle toward him, his arms extended like a great white pelican about to take flight—naked as a newborn rodent on a warm summer's eve.

Hair disheveled and a wide grin on his weathered face, Fred shambled down the aisle in a burst of energy. His steps were unsteady, but his eyes sparkled as he tottered forward, his arms flailing for balance. Despite his age, his spirit seemed youthful and carefree, his whoops echoing off the walls.

Alex laughed so hard his sides ached. "Now, why would you want to do something like that?" he asked, catching his breath.

"Because I can!" exclaimed Fred. He launched into a waltz routine that quickly turned into a cha-cha, his flabby body wiggling to a Latin beat only he could hear. Then he stopped abruptly. "Oh, no!" he cried in alarm.

"What's the matter now?"

"I think I just soiled myself."

Alex lowered his head sympathetically.

"I'll be right back." Fred shuffled off, head down.

"And don't forget to put your clothes back on!"

When Fred returned, he found Alex sitting against the pillar, sipping whiskey. "Follow me. I know where you can stay until the store opens tomorrow morning."

Alex followed, quietly considering whether to clear.

"I don't know how you plan on walking out of here tomorrow with that fancy coat, but I strongly advise against it. Maybe it's time to shape up and be a good soldier," Fred said, wagging his finger in the air. Their footsteps echoed off the walls in the absence of a reply. Abruptly, he stopped and snapped his fingers. "I know where I've seen those eyes. You were at my daughter's party!"

Fred spun around, but Alex was gone. A moment later, he heard a car engine roar to life outside, tires screeching away.

* * *

Monday, August 23, 2004.

Once she was sure Alex was sound asleep, Stacey tiptoed out of the bedroom. Driving north on Cedar Swamp Road to Glen Cove, the lavish homes lining the street by Old Tappan Park blurred past her window, unnoticed. Just after two in the morning, she let herself into Kathryn's house and disarmed the alarm. Quietly, she proceeded up the staircase, gripping a canvas bag in one hand.

Stacey had had enough of sleepless nights from suppressing her anger and bitterness. Although she knew it was unhealthy, she refused to tell Erik the truth, preferring that he continue believing their father had died of natural causes. If it had not been for her acquisitive mother, Bradley would still be alive today, sharing his life and contagious laughter. Kathryn had stripped away her daughter's joy in life. *Miserable bastards, they deserve each other! And as far as Alex is concerned, he can rot in hell along with her!*

Stacey's actions had nothing to do with his infidelity. She'd let go of that easily enough. What truly bothered her was his avaricious nature and his refusal to reject his life of crime. Her nose twitched with pride. Something it had never done before.

Her heart jumped when the bedroom door squeaked, and she held her breath as her eyes adjusted to the dim light. Kathryn sprawled on the bed with the satin sheet pushed aside, her face faintly illuminated by the nightlight. The reek and empty bottle on the nightstand suggested her mother had indulged in shots of tequila before calling it a night. Stacey crept deeper into the dragon's lair. She placed the canvas bag at the foot of the bed, pulled out a gas mask, and slipped it over her face, pulling the straps taut. A four-ounce squeeze bottle came out next. The warning beneath the skull and crossbones read: Danger. Do not handle without a respirator mask. Do not operate in a ventilated area. Do not inhale.

After her practice with a foam mannequin head, Stacey thought administering the lethal dust would be quick and easy. But the sight of Kathryn's face rekindled all her childhood fears and insecurities. Her hand trembled as the memory returned. She was sneaking into the kitchen for a cookie from the ceramic rooster jar, only to freeze at the sound of her mother's foot tapping in time with those caustic words: *What are you doing?* Since that day, Stacey had despised surprises. Even more so, her inability to respond to the relentless barrage of her mother's vitriolic questions.

Newly resolved, Stacey held the small bottle up to her mother's nose, squeezed on the inhale, and quickly pulled it away to prevent the fine particles from becoming airborne on the exhale. As she repeated the process, the dust penetrated her mother's lungs and clung to the moist lining of the bronchioles.

Fighting down the urge to leave before her mother woke up, Stacey's fingers slackened. As if at her mother's behest, the cap slipped from her fingers and landed on Kathryn's chest with a small bounce. Stacey held her breath, her eyes wide with fear behind the mask. A bead of sweat trickled down her back as her mother stirred in her sleep. Her first instinct was to bolt, but she remained frozen, listening to her own muffled breathing and trying to still the rising terror. Oh so gently she lifted the cap and resealed the container, breathing a sigh of relief. With the mask and empty bottle stuffed back into the canvas bag, she turned to make her escape.

"What are you doing?"

Stacey's heart jumped. *What do I say?* There was no excuse for being in her mother's bedroom at three in the morning.

Kathryn turned on her side, stretched one arm across the bed in her sleep, and murmured, "Aren't you staying tonight, Alex?"

Stacey left without a second thought.

Kathryn's death stunned the community. No one was more surprised than Alex. Not because of her untimely end, but because he hadn't yet located her jewels. Slumped in his leather chair, he slammed his fist against the armrest and seethed, cursing himself. "I should've looked harder," he said aloud. He stared at the ceiling light, searching for a solution.

Kathryn was more intelligent than she looked. She always seemed to be one step ahead.

Alex stroked his chin and bit his lip. If not for her bulldozer-like resolve, he would have lifted the emerald necklace by now. Oblivious to the monochrome movie flickering in the background, he stood up and began pacing back and forth, fists clenching and unclenching. *That necklace alone must be worth a quarter of a million dollars!* His eyes gleamed, and a wicked grin spread across his lips. "I'll have it soon enough," he said, nodding confidently before sinking back into the chair.

Kathryn never had the opportunity to exclude her daughter from the will. As a result, the eight-bedroom estate, the pharmaceutical company, and her precious stones were still bequeathed to Stacey, with Erik Foster left empty-handed. She trusted Stacey to look after her brother after the inheritance. Her rift with Erik was simply a power struggle she intended to win.

Just as her mother had surmised, Stacey was already preparing to transfer the company's majority ownership to him. And true to her word, she would allow Kathryn the dignity of being buried with her precious gems. When she described the extra-wide casket required to accommodate the extraordinary burial dress and jewels, Alex flipped.

"That's ridiculous! Everyone and their mother

will try to dig up the grave! Look at what happened to King Tut!" Alex said, waving his arms.

"I'm having a special metal shell made that will be welded shut once the casket is put in. It'll be impossible for anyone to break in without heavy equipment."

Alex grimaced, then took a deep breath. The plan sounded credible, but still . . . "Where are the jewels now?" he asked casually.

"Safe in an undisclosed location," she said with a knowing smirk. She had to give him credit for asking.

* * *

Tuesday, September 7, 2004. 11:00 a.m.

The funeral united the rich and powerful, including Fortune 500 executives and the governor of New York, with his lovely wife, who had visited the estate on multiple occasions while Bradley was alive. Guests had traveled hundreds of miles to see Kathryn and her spectacular gems laid out for the viewing.

Alex waited for a chance to slip a flashlight into

Kathryn's casket. His chance came when a middle-aged woman dropped her glasses and accidentally kicked them toward the security guard standing by the open casket. The guard leaned over with a wince and slowly straightened to return them. *Probably a herniated disk*, Alex thought as he stepped forward and leaned over the casket. *Thank you, Lady Luck!*

"Excuse me, sir," the security guard said, flexing his double-jointed finger.

Alex's heart skipped a beat as he gave the guard a blank stare.

"You're not allowed to cross the viewing ropes. Please stay put while I take inventory," the guard said, his nasal voice turning several heads.

Alex shrugged at the group now staring in his direction and gave a sheepish chuckle. "Certainly, my man. Be my guest. You can even frisk me if you wish. I just wanted to pay my respects properly." He lifted both arms, letting his black coat spread open to reveal his designer deerskin belt.

"That won't be necessary, sir," the guard said apologetically, shuffling in hurried emperor penguin steps.

Alex casually shifted his gaze from one curious mourner to the next, wondering if any of them had seen him drop the flashlight. He could see the polished chrome handle next to her thigh. If the guard lifted the right lid, he might discover the addition and ruin Alex's only chance to get to the jewels.

Focusing on Kathryn's hands, the guard counted the extravagant display of tennis bracelets and rings. Next, he turned his attention to the ruby earrings, emerald necklace, and profusion of jewelry arrayed at her sides. Alex's jaw was so tense he swore he could have bitten through steel chains. His teeth gleamed as his lips parted in a grimace, eyes fixed on the slender flashlight.

"The only thing remaining is the anklet," the guard said, placing his hand on the lid that shrouded Kathryn's legs. "This will only take a moment." The flashlight shifted when he partially raised the lid.

"Do you actually believe I could reach her ankles from here?" Alex asked.

"Oh, of course not," the guard said, letting the lid slip from his grasp. "I'm only doing my duty, sir."

"You take your job very seriously." Alex slung an arm around the guard's shoulders and gave a conspiratorial squeeze. "I'll make sure the family knows how competent and efficient you are."

Leaning askew to ease the pressure of his herniated disc, the guard resumed his place at the casket's head, then glanced at his watch when the funeral director strode in. "Viewing is over and the casket will now be closed. Please move to the chapel, just through that door," said the director, pointing. "The service will begin in fifteen minutes."

Sunlight filtered softly through long, sheer golden drapes that hung from ceiling to floor. About 250 guests entered quietly and packed the plain wooden pews facing the old, dejectedly silent organ. Stacey and Erik stood in the vestibule, receiving hugs and condolences from people they had never met. He was pleased to see the board of directors, who also shared their enthusiasm for his long-awaited return. "I'm sure Erik wouldn't have a problem leaving his prestigious teaching position," Stacey said, smiling for the first time that day. She left him with the directors and approached Alex, who walked in from the viewing room like a cat that had just eaten the canary.

"I think everyone's here, and the eulogy is about to begin," she said, a slight blush rising in her cheeks. "Everyone except my grandfather, that is."

"Is he okay?"

"Believe it or not, he's in jail right now. Of all moments to pull one of his stunts," she said, shaking her head. "He likes to push the limits. The problem is, he always gets caught, and this time I refused to bail him out to teach him a lesson."

Alex nodded with a sly smile. "Maybe it's time for your grandfather to shape up and become a good soldier."

Her jaw tightened at the asinine comment. "Really, Alex? Coming from you?"

He shrugged, wishing he could take it back, knowing full well she had every reason to be upset.

Disappointed, Stacey shook her head again. "I suppose you should take a seat up front with Erik. I'll join you after I gather the pallbearers," she told him as she stalked off.

Alex nodded and moved through the room,

charming each person he passed, though his thoughts were fixed on Stacey. *Something's different about her.* Those impassive eyes, the hard line of her jaw, that little twitch in her nose unsettled him. Now that Stacey had inherited everything, she reminded him of . . . Kathryn. Even her walk suggested wealth and power. *How far will she take it?*

Pastor Jim Atkinson looked out into the congregation, his smile widening as he greeted them. He was a well-dressed, well-mannered, handsome Black man who comforted friends and loved ones with his whimsical sermons. "She liked to go shopping at high-end department stores on weekends. Oh, and on Mondays, Tuesdays, Wednesdays, and Thursdays as well."

Alex didn't care for his jovial tone and shifted in his seat as he calculated his next move. *How am I going to clear into Kathryn's casket with Stacey hanging over me? I can't take any chances with so many people standing around. I'll have to clear from my car, away from prying eyes, so I can focus on the distance and safely clear back. Can I clear once the casket is covered with dirt? I'd better go before then.*

"Are you OK?" Stacey whispered.

"Huh?" Alex felt stupid for not noticing when she sat down.

"You should pay attention," she said softly. "It doesn't look good to daydream in front of the pastor."

Alex looked up at the pastor, who had apparently finished his homage to Kathryn and was now advocating for a revolution of values and ideas. "I challenge each of you to go out and practice the joy of brotherhood," Pastor Jim said, his tone serious. "Random acts of kindness create a good foundation for living and help eliminate loneliness and sorrow. We must live in faith and love to generate hope. Look to the world with an open heart and reach out to those who cannot stand on their own two feet." Pausing to sweep his gaze out over the crowd with satisfaction, his eyes fell on Alex, who squirmed under the scrutiny. "While we live in a world where money is king, evil will always exist. The least we can do is look after those less fortunate than ourselves . . .

"Let me repeat the sage words a friend once told me . . ."

A hush settled.

Jim raised his hands—not in spectacle, but in conviction—and let the silence speak.

Then, with quiet authority and the weight of a promise, he said, "It is time."

Stacey gave Alex a sharp nudge.

After the service, a man in a black trench coat and rugged cowboy hat held the reins on a pair of majestic black Friesians that led the way, their hooves clip-clopping a somber beat. The six pallbearers sat solemnly on the stagecoach's narrow seats. Each time the coach hit a bump or pothole, their bodies jerked in unison, and the wheels squeaked in protest, as if echoing the complaints of an aging door in desperate need of oil. Following the hearse to White Blossoms, a private woodland garden cemetery, a line of stretch limousines and luxury cars crept in a procession reminiscent of the death of a U.S. president.

As the mourners crowded around the gravesite, a trio of bagpipers played "Amazing Grace." Lowering the bulky casket from the carriage, the pallbearers trudged to the graveside in slow formation. Even more impressive than the elaborately carved casket was the six-ton excavator required to lower it into the custom-built metal sarcophagus. The grave had been dug wide and deep to accommodate the container's oversized dimensions. Welders lowered their masks and fired up their blowtorches, sealing the metal container in a cascade of flickering light. As the last sparks faded, the excavator let out a throaty snort, expelling a thick plume of black smoke from its upturned steel nostril. A beast of precision and power, it steadied its grip. Then it lowered Kathryn into the earth, her final resting place.

"This is the part I don't like about funerals," Alex whispered, kissing Stacey on the head and slipping out of his seat. He hoped she would not follow him during the critical part of the interment and was relieved, upon reaching his car, to see she had remained seated. *I worried over nothing. This will be easy after all. No different from when I cleared into the old freezer as a teen.* But this time, he was prepared. With the aid of his trusty flashlight, he could confidently clear in and out without raising suspicion.

Moments later, Alex concentrated on Kathryn's location, now eight feet below ground level. One second, he was in his car. The next, he was gone. Inside the pitch-black casket, the silence of the dead was different from the silence of the living. Being eight feet under entailed a level of self-awareness he'd never experienced, a sensation only the dead might understand. He became acutely aware of his breathing and heartbeat from a new perspective.

Struggling in the confines of the coffin, Alex's hand brushed against Kathryn's cold face. Wasting no time, he shoved her body aside and then felt along the silky lining, searching for the flashlight. His fingers grazed it, but just as he reached for it, he accidentally knocked it further from his grasp. His breath came slow and deep, shaky but determined. *Stay calm. Start from the beginning, slow and easy.* Pushing against the cushioned board above his head, he inched himself down, enabling him to grasp the flashlight.

He exhaled in relief.

Salivating, he brought the flashlight to his face and clicked the switch.

Nothing.

Shock swept through his body, quickly followed by violent trembling. He took a moment to calm down and tried the switch again.

Still, nothing.

"What the fuck?" he whispered, his hands now shaking in dismay. His heart pounded, echoing in his ears like an unrelenting drumbeat.

Alex flicked the switch rapidly several times, but the blackness remained undisturbed. "Wait, keep calm. Stay *calm!*" he blithered. "Check the batteries. Maybe they're in backward."

Beads of sweat rolled down his neck, soaking his already-stained shirt. With shaking fingers, he pulled off the battery cover and found an empty chamber. His heart sank—deeper than Kathryn's grave. Something had gone terribly wrong!

"It's not possible!" he screamed, tears stinging his eyes. "I put fresh batteries in last night!" He shoved against the casket lid and scrabbled wildly— first at the satin padding, then the unrelenting mahogany—but it didn't budge. Desperation tethered him to his post. He was a permanent prisoner in Kathryn's cold tomb, trapped with her rotting body. Alex screamed again and again, but the only answer was the thud of dirt being shoveled above him.

Let me out of here!

Someone let me out! I can't breathe!

Can anyone hear me?

Let me OUT!

Pleeeeeease!

Family, friends, and strangers offered their last condolences, dwindling until Stacey stood alone by the mound, reflecting on the events of the past two weeks. Losing herself among the twittering of birds and the fragrant scent of massed flowers, she smiled wryly at life's unexpected quirks. *Survival requires action, even if that means cutting people off or brushing them*

aside.

Stacey held her purse firmly and walked down the slope. The gentle breeze ruffled her hair as she paused next to a trash can and watched a cherry blossom tree's delicate petals drift by her. In the coolness of its shade, she reached into her bag and took out two AA batteries—the same ones she'd removed from Alex's flashlight while gathering the pallbearers.

The batteries lingered in her hand for a moment as she allowed memories of Alex to flit through her mind. Then she let them all go. They hit the bottom of the trash can with a kerplunk, an appropriate end to that chapter in her life. *Two problems solved with flawless execution*, she thought. *It's all over. I've learned my lessons well. I'm ready to move forward.*

Heartache from the past had oppressed and challenged her, but also shaped her into who she was now. Guilt and remorse were for the weak and foolish. As she headed to her car, a lingering group of young men eyed her, their thoughts unmistakable. She saw the dollar signs in their eyes and, in the style of her deceased mother, gave them a callous stare as a warning, her nose twitching. *Don't fuck with me or my emotions unless you want to end up in a suitcase somewhere deep in Death Valley.*

ACKNOWLEDGMENTS

As Clear As Night was written between 2006 and 2008, long before the emergence of AI-assisted writing tools. In 2024, the author embraced these innovations to enhance the manuscript through selective drafting and editorial refinement. This manuscript reflects a collaborative process between the author and AI-assisted, with all final decisions and narrative direction remaining solely the author's.

I want to thank my beta reader and copy editor, Carissa Schlafer, of Carissa's Editorial Services, and my line editor, Ginny Ruths, Touchstone Publications, whose constructive feedback strengthened the story. In addition, any shortcomings that remain in the book after the editorial process are my own.

Chapter art generated by AI
Cover character generated by AI
Cover design by Tea Jagodić

ABOUT THE AUTHOR

Edgar spent the formative years of his life in Southern California, attending private schools. As a teen, he enjoyed reading horror and science fiction novels that explored utopian and dystopian ideas. He often wondered how a utopian society would come about. As a young adult, he noticed that most utopian and dystopian novels introduce readers to an unknown future without explaining its origin. Inspired by this, he wrote a story about a pre-utopian society on the cusp of becoming a great nation. Combining his love for fantasy, action, and suspense, he brings you an action-packed story that paves the path to a utopia. "Pay close attention," he says. "House of Broken Bones is a puzzle."

Edgar now lives in Ontario, California. He is retired and enjoys traveling and meeting with social clubs for karaoke, dining, and other fun activities.

X: @EdgarJHern12748

OTHER TITLES
THE CLOWN AND THE CAREGIVER
(A SHORT STORY)

Hurry, hurry, step right into the haunting world of *The Clown and The Caregiver*, where the glittering lights of Milagro Circus mask a sinister web of sabotage and terror. When a series of harrowing accidents plague the circus in Abilene, Texas, the performers point fingers at Daniel Dewhurst, the enigmatic carpet clown. Meanwhile, an ancient evil lurks within the reflection of a circus mirror, manipulating those who dare to look too closely. This darkly intertwined tale of betrayal, malevolence, and karmic justice will leave readers questioning the thin line between victim and villain.

Collect all three covers.

OTHER TITLES
LIFEGIVER

(A SHORT STORY)

A turbulent birth in the Perseus spiral arm of the Milky Way sends a fragment of a dying star hurtling toward Earth. As the atmosphere strips away its outer layer, a lone flake drifts down into the heart of Miami's beachfront. In a twist of cosmic fate, young Herman Sinclair swallows the fragment and is forever changed.

Gifted—and cursed—with the power to bring inanimate objects to life with a touch, Herman's mother, Evelyn, works tirelessly to shield him from the public. For years, her vigilance keeps his abilities hidden. But when a moment of freedom in a bustling Miami mall sets chaos in motion, Herman's secret explodes into the open. This gripping tale of power, responsibility, and sacrifice probes the human cost of extraordinary gifts and the chaos unleashed by a single starry fragment.

Collect all three covers.

OTHER TITLES
HOUSE OF BROKEN BONES
(COMPLETE NOVEL)

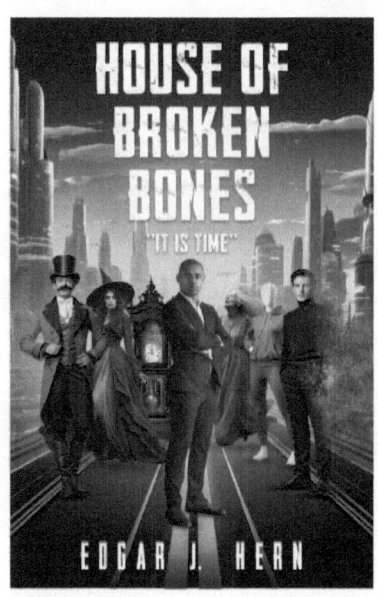

A collection of seven macabre and imaginative short stories that delve into the depths of human nature and the supernatural. From a man with the power to transport his physical body to a vengeful young woman who transforms into a wicked witch, these tales explore the extraordinary. A sinister circus plagued by sabotage, a grandfather clock with the ability to manipulate time, and a boy who breathes life into mannequins highlight the eerie and enigmatic. Additionally, a psychic girl fights to save the universe from implosion, and a provocative story examines the Senate's debate on eradicating money from society to combat the roots of evil. Each story is a piece of the puzzle, intricately interconnected to form a haunting tapestry.

www.ingramcontent.com/pod-product-compliance
Lightning Source LLC
Chambersburg PA
CBHW020542130626
46552CB00007B/2722